PAPA'S CHRISTMAS STORIES

Louis M. Krenz

authorHOUSE

AuthorHouse™
1663 Liberty Drive
Bloomington, IN 47403
www.authorhouse.com
Phone: 833-262-8899

Published by AuthorHouse 08/19/2022

ISBN: 978-1-6655-6783-1 (sc)
ISBN: 978-1-6655-6786-2 (e)

Library of Congress Control Number: 2022914638

Print information available on the last page.

CONTENTS

DEDICATION

*Dedicated to the grandchildren
of Louis and Karen Krenz.
In loving memory of our
parents and grandparents*

INTRODUCTION

Papa's Christmas Stories was written upon the birth of my first grandchild. When my first grandchild was born, I got the urge to write Santa's Lost Dog. When my second grandchild was born my daughter in law asked me "Where is his Christmas story?" This started a trend.

This book is written at the 3rd and 4th grade reading level. Yet younger children will enjoy the stories read to them and older children will enjoy reading them too. You will find that some of the characters will show up in the different stories. The stories were written in sequence from the oldest to the youngest of my first eight grandchildren. My grandchildren called me Papa. Thus part of the title.

SANTA'S LOST DOG

(Where did Santa's dog go on Christmas Eve?)
(Wess's Story)

This is a Christmas story,
for the time of year, we celebrate God's Glory.
It is just for Wess.
I hope he likes it, yes!

It was the day of Christmas Eve
and Santa was preparing to leave
to bring throughout the world toys
to all the good girls and boys.

It was a time for Santa to be glad.
Then why was Santa looking so sad?

Everyone seemed so busy. The elves were busy loading Santa's sleigh and harnessing the reindeer in preparation for Santa's trip.

Mrs. Claus was busy making Santa's lunch for his long trip and keeping snacks out for the elves as they went about their work. No one but Santa had noticed that Santa's dog Fleck was nowhere to be found

Santa had looked all around,
But no Fleck was to be found.

Each year Santa's dog Fleck would ride with Santa and keep Santa company on his long long trip around the world. As Santa would deliver the toys to all the girls and boys, Fleck would watch the reindeer and Santa's sleigh for him.

Santa was just a wreck.
Where was Fleck?
Soon Santa had to go,
but without Fleck Santa was feeling pretty low.

"Everyone look for Fleck," said Santa. They looked in Santa's kitchen, dining room, in the living room, under the Christmas tree and all-around Santa's house. But Santa's dog was nowhere to be found.

The elves searched the barn, the feed shed, the toy factory and the forest around Santa's house. Still no Fleck could be found. "Here Fleck! Here Fleck!" shouted everyone. But Fleck didn't answer.

"Did you look in the hay loft?" asked Santa, "Did you look behind the house? Did you look in the storage shed?". "We have looked everywhere", said Santa's helpers, "but we can't find Fleck."

Who would ride with Santa on this Christmas Eve?
Without his faithful dog could Santa leave?
What would Santa do with all those toys,
if he didn't deliver them to all the girls and boys?

Who would go and keep Santa company this night? Who would watch Santa's sleigh and reindeer while Santa delivered all the toys? Most important, who would make sure Santa did not fall asleep driving his sleigh all night or worse yet, make sure he did not forget some little girl or boy?

"I'll go," said Mrs. Claus. "No," said Santa "you must stay here to feed the elves and take care of things, besides the trip would be far too long for you to make."

"Take me along," said Johnny Elf, "I can help you!" "Thanks," said Santa, "but you and the other elves must stay here to clean up and start getting ready for next year. We must be sure to have enough toys for all the boys and girls next year too."

Santa gave a deep sigh,
as a tear came into his eye.
This will be the first in many a year
That the trip will be just Santa and his reindeer.

As Santa made his way toward his sleigh, he was feeling a bit lonely. He was missing Fleck. Santa had never made this long trip without his dog before. It will be a lonely trip without Fleck.

Just as Santa was about to climb into his sleigh, he thought he heard a bark. "Did you hear that?" asked Santa. "What?" asked the elves. "I guess I was just wishing for Fleck," Santa remarked.

But then, there it was again. Arf! Arf! Where was that noise coming from? It seemed to be from far away. It was Fleck's bark all right. But where could he be? "Here Fleck!" called Santa, "Here Fleck!"

The elves and all the reindeer
called "Here Fleck, here."
Up and down and on the ground
They looked for Fleck all around.

Then, as Santa peered into his sleigh looking up at him from between the toys, was a little black nose and two brown eyes. It was Fleck.

Fleck had fallen asleep at the bottom of Santa's sleigh and, unknowingly, the elves had covered Fleck with toys.

Now Fleck was awake and crawled out from under the toys ready to accompany Santa on his trip. A big smile crossed Santa's face, for Fleck would be going with Santa to deliver toys to all the girls and boys.

Well, what more can we say?
It will be a great Christmas day.
Fleck delivering all the toys,
to all the good girls and boys.

MERRY CHRISTMAS TO ALL
AND TO ALL A GOOD NIGHT

From Santa and Fleck
THE END

NO PRESENTS UNDER THE TREE

(A story about the Blue Angel)
(Brennan's Story)

Christmas story for the time of year,
when we celebrate Jesus' birth and spread good cheer.
Specially written for the first Christmas
of a little boy named Brennan.

Our story begins on a cold Christmas Eve. The snow was falling lightly and as the wind blew it whistled through the old farm house. Janne and her brother, Donny, wondered if they would have a Christmas this year.

Janne, Donny and their dog BeeZee helped their father cut a Christmas tree yesterday. It has always been a family tradition to go into the woods and find a tree for Christmas. It was a fun time.

They would walk with dad through the trees, then locate just the right tree. Dad would saw the tree down and they all would drag it out of the woods together.

Christmas Eve was when the family would prepare the tree. Decorating the tree was getting the house ready for the celebration of Jesus' birthday.

Mother had found in the attic the old worn-out Christmas decorations and Dad was setting up the tree in the living room. Then the whole family would decorate the tree together. Even BeeZee would be under foot as the family prepared the tree for Christmas.

When the tree was finally decorated, Janne and Donny were a little disappointed. The Christmas ornaments were so old and many of them were missing. The nice tree looked half empty.

Then Donny asked his mother, "Mom where are the presents that should go under the tree?" His mother replied, with a tear in her eye, "I'm sorry Donny, but there are no presents under the tree this year." Janne and Donny felt sad as they looked at the half-decorated tree with no presents under it.

Donny thought that maybe when Grandpa and Grandma came for Christmas dinner, they would have some presents to put under the tree. Mother broke up Donny's day dreaming when she said "OK kids, it's getting late and it is time for bed."

Janne and Donny were tired. The past two days had been pretty busy, so off to bed they went without any argument to stay up later. They climbed the steps of their two-story house.

On the second floor were two bed rooms, one for Janne and Donny, and one for their parents. They put on their pajamas and were soon fast asleep.

Donny was awakened by a bright light shining in the window. He got out of his bed and went over to Janne's bed. He poked Janne saying, "Janne, Janne, what's that bright light?" Janne said, "Leave me alone I'm trying to sleep."

Donny went over to the window to see what the bright light was. Janne asked Donny, "What do you see?" Donny replied, "A bright blue star." Janne then went to the window to see the star. Donny asked Janne, can you wish upon a blue star?" Janne said, "I don't know, I have never seen a blue star before."

As Janne and Donny sat by the window, BeeZee crawled up beside them. His nose poking underneath Donny's hand, BeeZee wanted Donny to pet him. As Donny was petting BeeZee, he said to Janne, "I'm going to make a wish. I'm going to wish for presents under the Christmas tree."

As soon as Donny made his wish, the blue star got brighter and brighter and brighter. It looked like the blue star was going to crash right through the window into their bedroom. Janne and Donny became frightened and started to back away from the window as the blue light got brighter.

The light was like a moon beam shining through the window, but it was blue instead of white. "I'm afraid," said Donny. Just then the whole room became bright blue. "Don't be afraid!" said a voice from behind them.

Janne and Donny turned around quickly to see who it was. "Who are you?" asked Janne. "I'm the blue angel of Christmas," replied the heavenly creature, "you made a wish upon me and I'm here to help make your wish come true."

She was a beautiful angel, with golden hair and a white flowing gown and was surrounded by a glowing blue light. Donny stood there frozen from shock. He had never expected his wish to come true.

"Come with me downstairs," said the blue angel, "and we will decorate your tree with my friends." "What friends," asked Janne. "You'll see", said the blue angel.

"Where's BeeZee?" asked Donny. They looked around the room and there was BeeZees nose poking out from under the bed. "He must have been frightened," said Donny

So, Donny, Janne, BeeZee and the blue angel proceeded down the steps to the living room. When they entered the living room what a surprise! It was full of everything. They saw:

Dasher and Dancer,
Prancer and Vixen,
Cupid and Comet,
Donner and Blitzen,

and Rudolph too.
BeeZee, he didn't know what to do.

There was the King and Queen of Hearts.
In the corner were elves playing darts.

All Donny could do was stare
as he watched decorating the tree, the
Christmas Bear.

There was big Elk and Moose,
and this silly little goose,
wrapping presents for under the tree.
Janne said "I hope there's a present for me."

BeeZee found Fleck, "That's Santa's dog you
know."
And there was this monkey on a pole.

There was scaredy dog and scaredy cat,
lying in a corner on a mat.
There was also Goldilocks,
and dressed so nice Miss Frilly Fox.

They all were decorating the tree,
even Big Bird, Bert and Ernie you see.
They saw Squeaky Squirrel with a peanut in
his jaw,
and a black crow singing Christmas carols,
hurrah.

There was a goblin named gotch,
and a mouse winding his watch.
Cleo Cow was there,
and so was Smokey the bear.

Everyone was singing and having fun
decorating the tree for God's son.
Janne and Donny pitched right in
and the blue angel watched with a big grin.

Wow! What a great time was had by all.
It was like having a great big spring ball.

The Christmas songs made a great sound
and stacks of presents were all around.
The tree looked lovely with its new ornaments
with bells, candy canes, ribbons and pendants.

"What a wonderful Christmas this will be
with Mom, dad, grandparents and me,"
said Donny. "Too bad Aunt Grace and Uncle
Ronnie couldn't be here."

"Donny! Donny! Donny!" cried mother,
"It's time to get up now. It's Christmas Day. Come on you
sleepy heads get out of bed."

Donny awoke rubbing his eyes. Was the blue angel just a
dream? Donny looked at Janne and smiled. Janne smiled
back. "I had this strange dream about a blue angel," Donny
told Janne. "That's funny," said Janne, "I had a dream like
that too."

All of a sudden Janne and Donny heard Dad from down stairs. "Hey, everybody come on down stairs and look at this," he said, "I can't believe what I see." Mom, Janne, Donny and BeeZee ran down the steps. There in the living room was the most beautiful Christmas tree you could ever imagine.

There were new ornaments, bells, candy canes, ribbons and pendants hanging about the tree. Under the tree were presents galore for Grandpa and Grandma, for mother and father, for Janne and Donny and even one for BeeZee.

"How did all this Happen?" asked Dad. Janne looked at Donny and just smiled. Mom looked at Dad and they just smiled too.

The End

BEST FRIENDS

(Can cats and dogs be friends)
(Camden's Story)

This is a special story;
To celebrate the Christmas glory.
Do you want to know what it is all about?

This story Is not about a rat.
Nor; is it about a big flying bat.
Maybe you have heard this story,
roundabout.

No, it is not about a funny hat.
But it is about a little scaredy cat.

This story is for you to hear,
because a boy named Camden did appear.
The story is told in the forest, so do not doubt!
So, hear the story and listen closely, throughout.

There is a place deep, deep, in the forest where only animals live. No person has ever found this spot. In this location on a bright sunny summer day, Mrs. Cat gave birth to four kittens.

The last kitten to be born was the smallest of the litter. He was born into a world that seemed very noisy. When he heard the cries of his brothers and sisters, he hid himself underneath his mother.

When he peaked out from underneath his mother, the bright sunlight fell upon his face. He was scared and crawled back underneath her. His mother laughed, and said, "Such a scaredy cat". From then on, all the animals called the little cat **"Scaredy Cat"**.

When mommy cat would go out and find food for the kittens, Scaredy Cat would cling to her. "Don't leave me," cried Scaredy. "Oh, for Pete's sake, don't worry," said the mother cat, "I will be back soon."

Then mother cat would go out into the forest. She always came back with lots of food for her kittens so they would grow big and strong. For someday she knew they would leave the forest for a home of their own.

When Scaredy Cat would hear thunder and lightning, he would run and hide in an old tree. All the animals teased Scaredy. They were mean to him. They would sneak up on Scaredy and frighten him. They would push him and laugh. The animals would holler and say;

"Scaredy cat, Scaredy cat,
frightened by a funny hat!"
"Scaredy cat, Scaredy cat,
frightened by a flying bat!"

Scaredy Cat did not like to be teased. It made him feel sad. Because he frightened easily, he would sneak around. He would hide behind trees and bushes.

When it seemed safe, he would peak out at the many things that were in the forest. He spent his summer exploring his new world. He would wonder off by himself and look at all the neat things in the forest.

He would watch the birds fly,
and he saw a willow tree cry.
"What is the matter Mr. Tree?"
Mr. Tree said, "I got stung by a bee".

He saw an ant working his farm,
but he did him no harm.
He followed a path somewhere,
as far as he would dare.

When he was hungry, he would stop and eat,
usually, he could find something sweet.
There were insects, leaves and berries.
In the trees he found apples and cherries.

It was fun wandering around,
in and out, up and down.

As Scaredy Cat grew older,
he became bolder and bolder.

Then one day while walking alone,
he slipped and fell on a dinosaur bone.
He fell down in the dirt,
but he did not get hurt.

A big owl went "Who, Who!"
So, what did Scaredy Cat do?
He ran into an old log
and there hiding was a dog.

"Yipe!" yelled, the dog in the log. "Help!" yelled, Scaredy Cat. Then Scaredy Cat shaking said, "Who, who, are you?" "They call me Scaredy Dog, because I hide from everything", came a nervous reply.

Then Scaredy Cat carefully walked toward Scaredy Dog. When he could see him eye to eye he grinned and said "They call me Scaredy Cat."

Scaredy Cat and Scaredy Dog became the best of friends right away. They begin playing and running through the forest together. It was great to have a best friend to share things with.

Scaredy Cat and Scaredy Dog never had a best friend before. They were having so much fun they forgot to pay attention to where they were.

They wandered deeper and deeper into the forest. Then they stopped and looked at each other. They realized at the same time that they were lost.

After looking at each other they started to laugh. For the first time in their lives, they were NOT scared. They had each other. **Best Friends!**

One day as they were walking through the forest a snow flake fell and landed on Scaredy Dog's black nose.

Scaredy Cat asked Scaredy Dog, "What is that?" "It is snow", said Scaredy Dog, "It is fun to play in".

As the snowflakes fell, Scaredy Cat and Scaredy Dog played. They played so hard they wore themselves out. Then they went over to a big tree to sit down to rest.

As they were sitting there, a jolly old man in a red winter suit and his dog came walking by. "What have we here Fleck", said the old man to his dog, "but a scraggly dog and a scraggly cat.

"We are not scraggly," said Scaredy Cat. "Yes," echoed Scaredy Dog, "We are just a lost dog and a lost cat." "That's right," said Scaredy Cat. "We do not have any place to live."

We have been living in the forest, under the trees and logs and in bushes." "Ho, Ho, Ho," said the jolly old man, "I know who you two are; You're Scaredy Cat and Scaredy Dog."

Well, that sure surprised Scaredy Cat and Scaredy Dog. "How did you know our names?" asked Scaredy Dog. "Oh, I know lots of things," said the jolly old man, "You might say I have a little bit of magic.

I think I can help you two find a nice home. I have a lot of boys and girls who would like a nice cat or dog just like you two", said the old man. The old man sat awhile, on the log, petting his dog, and talking with Scaredy Cat and Scaredy Dog.

"What is a boy or a girl," said Scaredy Cat. Because growing up in the forest, he had never seen a boy or a girl; so, the jolly old man explained to Scaredy Cat what it was like to live with people. "That sounds like fun," said Scaredy Cat. "Yup," said Scaredy Dog, "that does sound like fun".

"Come with me then," said the jolly old man. They followed the jolly old man as he went swiftly through the forest. They traveled so fast it was almost like magic.

"First we will go and tell your parents about your new homes," said the old man, "Then, we will be off to my house, to prepare for our trip to see all the little boys and girls."

On the way to the old man's house, they ran across Don Coyote. The old man called out;

> "Stop right there Don Coyote;
> who are you off to see?"
> Don stopped quickly on his paws.
> "Oh, it's you", said Don; "Santa Claus."

"Santa Claus!" said Scaredy Cat and Scaredy Dog,
as they came to a stop from their jog.
They said, spinning around and giving each
other a look,
"I thought Santa Claus was only in a book."

Don Coyote responded, "I'm off to see Miss Frilly Fox.
With her Christmas present in this box."
To the Blue Angels Christmas Party, I will go."
"We will stop by too," said Santa, "Ho, Ho, Ho."

Then Santa, Scaredy Cat and Scaredy Dog went on to Santa's house. When they finally arrived, they were very tired. They had a day they would never forget. They climbed up into Santa's sleigh and fell asleep.

When Scaredy Cat awoke, he found himself in a strange house. A little girl was petting him nicely. This made him feel warm all over. This must be the little girl that Santa had told him about. Scaredy Cat begins to play with her and discover his new home.

When he finished playing, he laid down for a rest and started to think about Scaredy Dog. This made him feel lonely. Would he ever see his best friend again?

As he lay there, he heard a little boy's voice outside and a dog barking. Scaredy sprang up to the window ledge so he could see outside. There, to his surprise in the neighbor's yard, just next door, was Scaredy Dog playing in the snow with his new friend.

As Scaredy Cat pressed his face against the window, Scaredy dog ran over and wagged his tale. **"Best friends forever?"** asked, Scaredy Dog. Scaredy Cat grinned, the only way a cat could grin, and said, **"BEST FRIENDS."**

THE END

4

INSIDE OUT CHRISTMAS

(Santa's Christmas Eve Party)
(Allyn's Story)

There was a little girl to be,
born in October of 1993.
You heard the grandma's shrill,
for them it was the greatest thrill.

So, another Christmas story to be told.
Remember the gifts of myrrh, frankincense,
and gold,
Given to a baby of long ago,
who was born in a manger so low.

This new story you may not believe,
But it happened late on Christmas Eve.
Now listen! So, I don't have to shout,
About a world that is; ***inside out.***

It was a cold snowy Christmas Eve. Santa was making his next to last stop at the Zeez house. He was tired. It had been a long night delivering toys to all the girls and boys.

There were some cookies and juice on a table by the Christmas tree. Santa saw them and decided to sit for a moment. As he sat, he mumbled out loud, "Only one more stop to make after this one".

Santa never took time to sit on Christmas Eve. He had to keep his magical sleigh and reindeer in supersonic speed to make sure he delivered toys to all the boys and girls.

Well, since he was almost done delivering his toys, he thought it would be Ok to take a moment to rest. He helped himself to the cookies and juice.

Unknown to Santa, hiding behind a door, were Bethany and Stephen., two of the Zeez children. All of the Zeez children were named after names in the Bible. The other children were; the twins, James and John, Paul, the oldest, Mary, and the baby Diana.

When Bethany and Stephen saw Santa sitting for a moment, they slipped outside. There they saw Santa's magical sleigh and his nine reindeer; You know, Dasher and Dancer, Prancer and Vixen, Cupid and Comet, Donner and Blitzen, and of course, Rudolph too.

There on the seat sleeping was Santa's dog, Fleck. Bethany and Stephen moved closer to Santa's sleigh. The sleigh was a lot bigger than they had thought. They went right up to it, crawled up the side, and peeked inside. To their surprise the sleigh was empty!

"But I thought I heard Santa mumble he had one more stop to make?" said Stephen to Bethany! Then they heard some bells coming. "It's Santa coming!" said Bethany. "What should we do?" asked Stephen. "Quick hide!" said Bethany. They both jumped inside Santa's sleigh and hid themselves in a corner.

Santa was tired, after his long night's work, and did not pay any attention to the two little children cuddled together in the corner of his sleigh.

Soon the magical sleigh and reindeer were off the ground and flying at a speed that frightened Bethany and Stephen. They clung tight to each other in a corner of Santa's sleigh. Like lickety-split, they were in the clouds. Before you could say Merry Christmas, they were dropping rapidly from the clouds back down to earth.

As the sleigh dropped from the clouds it was a warm sunny day. Quite different from the snow and cold that Bethany and Stephen had left. When they landed there was a crowd of people to greet Santa.

Santa jumped down from his sleigh. "Here Fleck," called Santa, but Fleck stood on the seat barking and looking inside the sleigh. "What is the matter", asked Santa. Fleck barked again.

Santa crawled back up on to the sleigh to see what was the matter. As he peered into the sleigh, he saw two frighten little children curled up in the corner. "What have we here?", asked Santa. Bethany and Stephen had never been so frightened in their lives!

They were in a strange place and what was Santa Claus going to do with them. Stephen said, "I wish I would have gone to bed like mother told us to do, instead of sneaking downstairs and hiding behind that door."

"Ho, Ho, Ho," laughed Santa, "I see we have ourselves two little stowaways". "Come here," said Santa to Bethany and Stephen. Bethany and Stephen moved slowly toward Santa. They were very scared. What was Santa going to do to them?

"You need not be afraid" said Santa, "even though it was wrong of you to stowaway on Santa's sleigh". Santa could never harm a little child, or anything, because Santa only does good things.

As Bethany and Stephen crawled out of Santa's sleigh, they were shocked at what they saw. Santa's red suit had turned white with red trim and everybody else had their clothes on backwards.

"Ho, Ho, Ho," laughed Santa as he saw the surprised look on Bethany's and Stephen's face. "Do not be so surprised at what you see," said Santa, "for you have landed **in Inside Out Land."**

Santa laughed again, "Ho, Ho, Ho,
here meet this little boy named Bo.
He will tell you all about,
this land of inside out."

Where the sun is so bright,
it shines during the night;
and the moon comes out during the days.
So many things are done here in different
ways.

Like, clothes are worn inside out,
and you never heard anyone shout!
Things in the stores have no price,
and the weather is always nice.

It doesn't seem real,
they have dessert first, at every meal,
and play in the dirt instead of sand.
in this Inside Out Land."

Bo took Stephen's and Bethany's hand and they started
walking through Inside Out Land. Everything was so
strange. They saw swings that went sideways. A teeter totter
that went in a circle, like a merry go round.

In Inside Out Land crooked was straight and straight was
crooked. You lived in your yard and played in your house.
Dogs were cats and cats were dogs. Trains would fly and
planes would run on tracks. It was very confusing.

People would drive on the sidewalks and run and fly on the streets. **Fly? Fly on the Street!** "How can people fly?" Stephen asked Bo. "It's easy," said Bo. "You just take two steps, like this, and jump." Bo took two steps and floated across the ground. He looked just like a man walking on the moon.

Then Stephen thought he would try it. "You mean like this?" said Stephen, as he took two steps, and jumped into the air, but Stephen just fell flat on his face. Bo and Bethany Laughed! "You looked funny", said Bo, "I guess it takes some practice".

"Look over here", said Bethany. "What's that sign say?", Bethany asked Bo. It was hard to read because all the words and letters are backwards.

S'ATNAS EVE
YTRAP
GNIBR STFIG

"What does it mean?
Santa's Eve Party Bring Gifts!"
Stephen asked Bo.

Bo looked at Stephen with a confused look. "It's Christmas Eve when all the people give Santa presents. Don't they do that where you live too?"

Before Bethany and Stephen could answer they were interrupted by Santa. "You kids must have been having a great time since you missed the party", said Santa. Santa looked at Bethany and Stephen and said, "You see why I like this land"! Everyone is so nice here. They give me presents. What a great way to end my long, long night".

"Come on now it is time to go", said Santa, "enough of inside out land. Your parents and family are waiting for you," Santa continued, "I called them so they would not worry about where you were."

"But, Santa", asked Bethany, "the time here has been too short. Can't we stay longer?" "I'm sorry," said Santa, "but we must go. I need to get back to the North Pole to start working on next year's Christmas. It's time to say good bye to Bo and all our friends here at Inside Out Land."

While Bethany and Stephen were saying good bye to all their new friends, Santa was unhooking Dancer, Prancer and Blitzen from his sleigh. Then he talked to Rudolph and Fleck. He told them to take the sleigh back to the North Pole and he would join them later.

Santa put Bethany on Dancer, Stephen on Prancer, and Santa mounted Blitzen. "Get ready", said Santa to Bethany and Stephen, "for a great ride home". "Up Blitzen! Up Dancer! Up Prancer!" said Santa, and up went the reindeer with Santa, Bethany and Stephen on their backs.

Like magic they flew into the air, they went over fields and mountains, streams and forests, trees and towns, in and out of the clouds. They moved so fast it was like a blur.

In no time at all they had landed on the Zeez's front yard. There at the front door waiting were Bethany's and Stephen's parents, brothers and sisters. Their family was all excited to hear about their adventure.

Bethany and Stephen ran up the side walk eager to tell everyone about their trip to Inside Out Land. When they turned around to say good bye to Santa and the reindeer, they had already disappeared. In the distance they heard;

MERRY CHRISTMAS TO ALL

THE END

THE DAY THE TREES STOOD STILL

(A story about walking trees)
(Kara's Story)

A long, long, long, time ago,
before the time of snow,
when animals could talk,
and trees could walk,

in the valley oh so low,
a day in July that did glow,
and all the kingdom did celebrate
a princess's birth, it was great.

She was destined for fame
and Princess Kara was her name.

In the middle of a beautiful valley was a huge castle. This was where Princess Kara was born and grew up. To enter the castle, you had to cross a drawbridge because the castle was surrounded by a lake of water called a moat.

Inside the Castle there was the great court with a large room for festivals. Pageants, plays and parades all took place in the great court. Amusement was provided by the king's clowns who juggled and did acrobatics. The kings' magicians preformed magic.

There would be musical concerts by minstrels. They used a violin, harp, guitar, bagpipe, flute, horn trumpet, drum, tambourine, cymbals, hand bells, and there was an organ with pipes of gold. The great court was the most elegant in all the land.

Traveling musicians and merchants all wanted to stop by the castle. Here they could perform or show the king their goods. But really, they wanted to see the great court and quench their thirst from a fountain of wine that was in the corner.

It was exciting when traveling musicians and merchants came to town. It usually meant a celebration and every visitor had to tell the king a story.

On the castle walls were large cannons. In the middle of the castle was a small church called, "The Little Chapel of the Valley".

An old wise monk lived in the tower of the chapel where he prayed and fasted every day for peace in the valley. Because of his prayers the cannons on the castle walls never had to be used.

There was a barn yard where the animals; goats, sheep, pigs, chickens, ducks and geese lived. Princes Kara liked to visit the animals in the barn yard. Except for the geese, Princes Kara got along well with the animals.

Her favorite animals were the Arabian horses. On Saturday afternoon, Sunday's and holiday's, the governor of the valley made a law that nobody could work in the valley.

After the mid-day meal, on Saturday, everyone would have fun relaxing and playing games. This was usually followed by music and dancing in the evening.

On Sunday, a friar from the valley, came to the chapel and provided a church service for the King, his family, the knights and the squires.

The older people liked to walk around the village, that surrounded the castle, and visit with each other. The younger people liked to dance and dress up in gorgeous clothing and go on picnics in the meadows. Princess Kara enjoyed going on picnics the best.

Many young maidens from the valley would come to the castle to learn how to manage a household, housewifery, nursing, and learn to play music.

After their daily lessons were over the girls would play checkers, chess, backgammon, badminton, and sing songs

31

in harmony. Sometimes Princess Kara would be invited to play and sing with the older girls.

Princess Kara's most favorite room in the castle was the Great Toy Room. The King had the room made just for his princess. It had all the toys a girl could want.

There was a special courtyard garden in the castle with a fishpond surrounded by pretty flowers; lilies, roses, marigolds, poppies, violets and grape vines.

Living in the garden were beautiful birds; peacocks, parrots, flamingos and swans. Other birds like magpies, larks and jays would fly in and visit with the peacocks, parrots, flamingos and swans. It was the nicest garden in the castle.

Princess Kara liked to lie on the soft green grass in the garden court yard. On a warm, clear, night she would watch the stars. She would always see a falling star and would make a wish. Sometimes her wishes came true, but, sometime they did not.

As she lay in the garden she would dream about distant lands and would imagine what these lands would be like. The garden was one of Princess Kara's favorite places because it had an orchard.

The King had a special orchard made and invited the best fruit trees in the valley to come and stay. The King's favorite fruit trees would provide the King with the sweetest fruit in all the land.

There was a variety of fruit trees in the King's orchard bearing oranges, almonds, olives, apples, cherries, peaches and pears. The king provided the trees with a special Pruner that would take care of them. She would trim their branches and leaves when needed and doctor them for diseases when they got sick.

Princess Kara enjoyed visiting the orchard often. She liked walking with the trees through the garden especially the baby trees. Sometimes the pruner, if the trees said OK, would let Princes Kara help with the pruning.

It was a nice feeling being friends with the trees. Princes Kara liked being in the orchard when the birds came to make music for the trees. The trees would reward the birds with their fruit for singing to them.

Surrounding the castle was a small village. Princess Kara would walk down the brick streets and visit with the shop keepers. The shop keepers liked to see Princes Kara coming because she had such a lovely smile and pleasing personality.

They all enjoyed talking with the princess. There was the blacksmith who made gates, shields and things of iron, the tinsmith who made dishes of pewter, silver and gold and plates and cups of tin. There was the candle maker, the hat maker, the shoe maker, and the baker.

There was a chemist who made medicines, a carpenter shop where tables, chairs, beds, and many household things were made, and a stable where visiting animals could stay.

In the center of the village was an open market where peddlers would sell their goods each day. Gardeners would sell vegetables. Many tradesmen would sell their goods of leather, linens, blankets, crafts and other items people could use.

In the middle of the open market was a place where the scholars and philosophers would discuss worldly topics. The best part was when the story tellers would tell stories of times long, long ago.

Princess Kara always liked to hear these stories. Each night a Town Watchman would walk around the village and check to see if everything was alright. If he found that all things were well, at 7:00, he would sound a horn to say that all is well.

One day the great sequoia, monarch of all the trees, paid a visit to the fruit trees in the King's garden. The great sequoia demanded that the fruit trees leave the garden, so he, his cousins, and their families, could move into the garden.

The fruit trees refused and pushed the great sequoia out the castle's door and into the castle's moat. This made the great sequoia very, very mad.

The next day the great sequoia and his top aid, Redwood, made a call on the king. They threatened the king and said if he did not remove the fruit trees from the garden the great sequoia was going to call his evergreen cousins together and destroy the valley.

The great sequoia wanted the king to give him control of the King's castle, his garden and all the fruit trees. The king did not know what to do. There had never been any trouble in the valley before. What was going to happen to the valley?

The great sequoia gave the king one week to make a decision. He and Redwood then started to call together the evergreen families.

There was the spruce family; Norway pine, Serbian and Colorado, Douglas, white, the cedar family; and, the cypress's;

The evergreen families gathered together near a bend in the valley's river. As they united, they became so thick that they trampled the flowers, grass, wheat and hay in the fields leaving only dirt and sand in their path.

As the evergreens gathered, the people of the village became afraid. They looked toward the king for protection. The king gathered his knights and they prepared to do war with the evergreens. But the king did not want to do war with the evergreens.

In desperation the king of the valley sent a messenger to his brother, the king of the mountains, to bring his knights to the valley to join his brother. The king of the valley hoped that a great show of strength by the kings would discourage the great sequoia from starting a war.

When the king of the mountains received the message, he gathered his knights, and with his son, Prince Reed, went to the valley to help his brother.

By the time they arrive in the valley things had already gotten out of hand. The evergreens were running wild and trampling over anything in their way.

When they arrived in the castle, the king of the valley told his brother what had happened. How the evergreen and fruit trees of the valley had been fighting now for three days. The fruit trees of the valley had tried to stop the evergreens, but were failing. Everything was in a big mess!

The people of the village had moved behind the castle walls for protection. The king of the valley was a peaceful man and did not want to get involved in the fight. It would only end up harming more people and animals. What was the king going to do?

Princes Kara and Prince Reed were very concerned about the Tree War. They climbed up the stairs to the walkway on the castle wall so they could see what was happening in the valley.

There were tree limbs and leaves all over. It looked like a tornado had come through the valley. After they had looked over the wall they ducked down. It was just too freighting to look at.

"We must do something", said Princes Kara. "What can we do", said the Prince, "we are just two little kids." "I know!"

said Princes Kara, "Let's go and ask the wise monk in the chapel tower for help". "But he won't see anybody", said the Prince. "Yes, but he will talk to you" replied, Princes Kara, "I have talked to him before".

Princes Kara and Prince Reed went to the chapel, climbed the stairs to the tower, knocked on the tower door, and asked the wise monk for help. After they waited awhile, an answer came from behind the door. "Only God can stop this War," said the voice. "Now what do we do?" asked Prince Reed. "I Know! said Princes Kara, "Come on and follow me."

Prince Reed followed the princess down the stairs to the chapel. Here she said a prayer, "God please help stop this war between the trees". Then she waited, but nothing happened. Princess Kara asked God again. "God, we need your help," she prayed.

Then she waited again, but nothing happened. Now, Princess Kara was getting mad because God was not doing anything to stop the Tree War. Finally, as a last resort, she let out a yell that echoed throughout the valley, "**God Help!**"

Well; nothing happened and the prince and princess returned to the main rooms of the castle. They were tired after a very long day and both retired to their bedrooms to sleep.

The next morning, when everyone woke, it was still very dark. During the night a dense fog had settled in over the valley. It was so dense nobody could to go outside. Everyone had to stay inside. It was kind of fun though, because, everyone was playing games and it became a festive time.

It was a needed break after all the trouble everyone was having with the Tree War. The young people preformed pageants and plays.

The king's clowns juggled and did acrobatics, the king's magicians preformed magic, and a musical concert was performed by the village minstrels.

The dense fog continued for three days and three nights. Princes Kara and Prince Reed headed for the garden to play. When they got to the garden, they were stunned at what they saw.

All the trees stood still. They were stuck in the ground. Princess Kara and Prince Reed headed for the garden to play. When they got to the garden, they were stunned at what they saw.

All the trees stood still. Princess Kara and Prince Reed ran to the castle wall to look out over the valley. There in the valley all the trees stood still too. They were all stuck in the ground. None of the trees could move.

Princes Kara and Prince Reed realized that if the trees could not move, then they could not fight. The Tree War was over. From this day on all trees have been fastened into the ground and have never been able to walk again.

Fruit trees had to give their fruit to any person, animal or bird that could pick it. All trees had to stand in the sun and provide shade for the other animals and people on the earth.

The kings declared a holiday to celebrate the end of the Tree War. The king of the valley sent forth a decree throughout the land;

Each year from now on, to celebrate the peace, and because the evergreens started the war, each family will cut down an evergreen tree and decorate it to remind us of peace. Many people today still celebrate the peace on Jesus' birthday by decorating an evergreen tree reminding us to **Pray for Peace on Earth.**

THE END

THE DAY THE
SNOW BEGAN

(When animals could talk)
(Reed's Story)

A long long long time ago,
before the time of snow,
when animals could talk
and trees could walk,

in the mountains very high,
on a sunny day in July,
there was playing of a great horn,
when the new prince was born.

The King and Queen agreed,
to name the new baby, Prince Reed.

Prince Reed was born and grew up in a castle. The castle was made of large stones and located on a high rocky mountain in a remote part of the world.

The mountains would stretch up so high some times that they would touch the clouds. It was a land where people and animals helped each other, a very special and peaceful land.

In the castle where Prince Reed grew up, there was a large store house for food, a barn yard for animals, and a room filled with money, jewels and gold. There were large winding staircases that seemed to lead to nowhere and fireplaces in every room. It had deep cellars, underground dungeons and hidden passages where spies and messengers could sneak in and out of the castle unnoticed.

There were many courtyards within the castle for the noble household to use. The center courtyard had a big watermill which supplied water for the castle and moved a giant stone that would grind grains into flour for making breads and cereals.

Each day the servants would carry water from the watermill to a large water tank in the castle tower. This tank provided running water through bamboo stems to rooms in the castle.

It was lonely for the prince because there were no other children in the castle to play with. The king would not let the prince go outside the castle unless he was surrounded by the king's knights. The king thought it was dangerous for the prince to be in the mountains alone.

So; Prince Reed would play with the castle clowns and magicians. He learned acrobatics from the clowns and magic from the magicians. It was not much fun playing with adults all the time.

Each day the prince had to go to school. There, the scholars would teach the prince grammar, logic, music, math and astronomy; which is studying the stars.

Many young men came to the castle to learn how to be the king's knights. Sometimes the young knights would let the prince join them. The knights would teach Prince Reed how to ride horses, use weapons, swim, box and how to fence with a sword.

Mid-day dinner was at 11:00 in the morning. Prince Reed's favorite dessert was fresh bread and butter with pudding poured over it. It was delicious. After dinner the knights would rest by playing backgammon and chess. After they had rested, they would practice being knights and have tournaments.

Sometimes the older knights would have jousting tournaments. That is where two knights on horseback would oppose each other with weapons to see who could knock down the other knight first.

As Prince Reed grew older, he would spend his days wondering around the castle. He would watch the servants working and the young men who came to the castle to learn how to be knights.

At times he would just wander the great castle hallways and look at all the stuff: the armor, clusters of lances, shields, battle axes, and coats of arms that hung on the walls like pictures. There were also lots of paintings and sculptures all about the castle too.

Prince Reed liked to play about the many things that he found around the castle. He would pretend he was a great knight fighting off mean dragons.

One day while he was playing, he grabbed a lance off the wall. Suddenly the stone wall began to move. Prince Reed jumped back in fright. The wall opened up.

Prince Reed stared into the opening. All he could see was dark nothing. He then looked up and down the hallway to see if anyone else was around. There wasn't anyone else to be found. Not knowing what to do, the prince returned the lance to the wall. The wall closed as quickly as it had opened.

The prince thought about the opening in the wall for several days, then he got up the courage to go and remove the lance from the wall again. As before, all he could see was dark nothing. He opened and closed the door in the wall for several days and each time it was the same, dark nothing.

Several months went by and the prince could not stop thinking about the opening in the wall. Then one day he decided what he was going to do. He went to the candlestick maker and asked him to make a big candle that could burn for hours, because, Prince Reed had decided to enter into the dark opening in the wall.

The candlestick maker made him the candle. Prince Reed hid it in his room for several days as he worked up the courage to light it so he could look into the dark opening in the wall.

Finally, the day had come. This would be the day the prince would light the candle and look deeper into the opening in the wall.

The prince walked slowly to the place where the wall would open. His stomach felt uneasy because he was still afraid of going into the wall, but he kept on going anyway. He finally reached the place where the lance was on the wall. He quickly grabbed the lance.

He was afraid if he paused to think about what he was about to find in the opening in the wall, he would not follow through with his plan. The wall opened.

Prince Reed lit his candle and started walking into the opening in the wall. The first thing he saw was a narrow passage. He followed the passage along the back of the stone wall. It led to a stairway that went down.

It was so dark you could not see the bottom of the steps. Prince Reed's heart was beating fast as he begins to descend the stairs with only the candle light showing the way. When he reached the bottom of the stairs, he found a damp cave.

He started to follow the dirt floor of the cave as he walked further into the dark nothing. "Who's there?" came a voice from within the dark nothing. "What's that light?" came another voice from the dark.

Prince Reed froze, he was so scared he could not move or talk. All kinds of thoughts went through Prince Reed's head. Were these dragons that were about to devour him? Were these monsters of the mountains that would make a slave out of him? Oh..., right now Prince Reed wished he was back in his room and in his warm bed.

"It's a little boy" came the voice again. "What is a little boy doing down here!" came the other voice. "What's your name?" asked the first voice. Prince Reed tried to overcome his fright.

As he regained his self-control, he thought, I am a prince, I will not be frightened. He then answered the voices in the dark. "I am Prince Reed, prince of the castle above," he replied, and he asked, "Who are you?"

"I am Desmo and this is my brother Rufus. We are the batmasters of this cave" came the reply. Prince Reed turned his candle toward the sound of the voices and there sitting on a ledge were two bats.

"What is a batmaster?" asked Prince Reed. "We take care of the cave and make sure no harm comes to anyone while they are in the cave" responded Desmo.

It suddenly dawned on Prince Reed that he was talking to an animal. "How is it that you can talk? asked the prince. "Why? Don't you know? All animals can talk." replied Rufus. "I didn't know that!" said Prince Reed.

Well! responded Rufus, Have you ever tried to talk to an animal?" Prince Reed thought for a moment, "No, I guess I haven't." "Well!" came back Rufus, "If you would take the time to talk with animals you would have known that we can talk."

The prince talked with Desmo and Rufus for a long time. Then they showed him around their cave. Prince Reed was introduced to the other animals that shared the cave with Desmo and Rufus.

There was; Pinky Possum, he was called Pinky because he had a pink nose. Frisky Fox, who was always wanting to race everybody. Stinky Skunk, you know why he got his name. Brownie Bear, who of course was brown.

Don, the deer, named after his grandfather and Whitey, the deer, named because of his white tail. Ronnie Rabbit, who was always finding things to eat. Windy Mouse, because he was always winding his watch. And, a goblin named Gotch, all shared living in Desmon's and Rufus' cave.

Then they came to the outside opening of the cave and the prince got his first real look at the mountains. Before he only saw the mountains by looking over the castle walls.

Don and Whitey deer showed Prince Reed around the mountains and introduced him to the mountain animals. After this day Prince Reed made several trips a week to the cave and the mountains below the castle.

He became friends with the animals in the cave and the animals of the mountains. They were all fun to play with, a lot more fun than the adults in the castle.

One day as Prince Reed sat on the grass, in the garden court, and was visiting with the birds, he heard the ground rumbling from the feet of a lot of horses. He ran to the castle walls and climbed up to look out to see what was all the noise. There, coming down the main road to the castle, was the king's brother, the king of the valley, and all his knights.

Prince Reed wondered if his cousin, Princess Kara, princess of the valley, was with his uncle and their party. Prince Reed enjoyed his uncle's visits, for they were always festive times and when Princess Kara came along, he had another child to play with.

The Prince was excited when he saw Kara. He couldn't wait to tell and show her the secret cave he had found in the wall. He thought to himself; "Won't she be surprised when I show her the cave?"

After his uncle and his party arrived inside the castle it did not take Prince Reed long to find his cousin, Kara, and tell her all about his adventures in the cave and the mountains. Soon they were both at the wall.

The prince grabbed the lance from the wall and exposed the dark opening to Kara. He lit his big candle and they proceeded down the staircase to the cave. When they reached the cave, the prince called out for the bat masters, Desmo and Rufus.

"Desmo! Rufus! Where are You?" There was no answer. The Prince called again, "Desmo! Rufus! Where are you?", and again there was no answer. As Prince Reed and Princes Kara walked through the cave not one animal could they find.

"Maybe they're all out in the mountains," said the prince. So, they made their way to the mountain opening of the cave. "Anybody here?" shouted Prince Reed.

"Anybody here?" shouted Princess Kara. Princess Kara could shout a lot louder than Prince Reed, but still nobody answered.

"Psst", came a small voice from behind a rock, "Psst". Prince Reed turned around and he saw Stinky Skunk hiding behind the rock. "What's the matter?" asked the Prince.

"Shh; quiet," said stinky, "come over here behind the rock". Prince Reed and Princess Kara went over behind the rock where stinky was hiding. Stinky told the prince and princess all about why the animals were hiding.

Two days ago, some men, called hunters, entered the mountains. When the animals went up to welcome them, some were shot with the hunters bow and arrows.

The rest of the animals then ran and hid. Stinky also told them that the animals were not talking to people anymore because they were afraid for their lives. This was a sad day in the mountains.

"Hunters are coming," said Stinky, as he ran further back into the rocks to hide. Those were the last words any animal ever spoke. Just then Don and Whitey Deer came running by. They were being chased by the hunters.

Prince Reed ran out to stop the hunters, but, as the hunters came by, they just pushed the prince aside and kept chasing the deer. The prince and princess screamed for the hunters to stop but nobody would listen.

"Oh God Help!" shouted Prince Reed. Suddenly a big wind came up and dark clouds rolled out from within the mountains. It began to thunder and lightning. Was the world coming to an end, thought Prince Reed. It was very scary.

Then it began to rain. Soon it started to get colder and colder. Then something happened that had never happened before. The rain changed into white crystals. As the white crystals fell from the sky, they formed a layer of white covering the mountains

Prince Reed bent over and picked up a hand full of crystals to see what they were like. They looked like flakes of grain and felt soft like linen. "What is this?" asked Princess Kara. Let's name it SNOW, said the Prince.

S - for **S**tinky and all the animals.
N - for **N**o more hunting on the king's land
O- for **O**nce there was peace between people
  and animals and
W - for the **W**hite of its color.

Then they heard some confusion off in the distance. They turned around to see what it was. The hunters seemed to be very confused and were wandering in circles.

Then Prince Reed and Princess Kara saw why the hunters were so confused. Not only had God created something new in the white crystals, we call snow, as Prince Reed and Princess Kara watched, Don and Whitey Deer turned white in color and blended right into the snow.

Many other animals' their fur was turning white also. Frisky Fox, Pinky Possum, Brownie Bear, Ronnie Rabbit, and even Windie Mouse all turned white.

To help make up for the cruelty of the hunters, Prince Reed and Princess Kara wrapped up some presents for the animals and left them at the opening of the cave to the mountains.

After that day Prince Reed never entered the cave again. Many people today still give animals presents at the time of year we celebrate the birth of Jesus. And, when it snows many people set out food for the animals and birds to help them through the winter

Today many animals are white or turn white when it snows to remind us of the day when animals stopped talking and *THE DAY THE SNOW BEGAN.*

THE END

7

ALPHA FAMILY CHRISTMAS

(Is there really a Santa Claus?)
(Kieran's Story)

This story was written in Kokomo.
In the season of the mistletoe.
The year of a baby's birth by Papa K
to celebrate the joyous Christmas day.

That day of Jesus Birth,
who came to save our sinful earth.
This new story are you ready to hear?
If so; how about a nice big cheer!

Far, far away,
in the land of **A**,
in the county of **Z**,
there lived the Alpha Family.

Now in the land of **A**
when you talk you must say,

everything in rhyme
from early morn to bedtime.

When you write
it is quite a sight.
For you see every time,
it is written in rhyme.

That's right, in the Land of **A**
the language rules you must obey.
For everyone talks in rhyme you see.
So, in rhyme this story will be.

Let's see, how shall we start?
I know, let's make a family tree chart.
There are 26 members in the ALPHA family.
This way each one you will get to see.

There are nine
members that rhyme
you know; **B, C, D, E, and G.**
Followed by **P, T, V,** and **Z.**

There are the twin rhymes too.
The ones that work in the zoo
are the brother's **J** and **K.**
They live together by the bay.

The other twin rhymes **I** and **Y**
are the ones who never say goodbye.
They are very, very shy.
But they always say HI!

First, so you will not doubt
there are another 13 members about.
Let us take the time to learn to know
each member like a picture show.

We shall start at the beginning.
Some verses will leave you grinning.
Others will send you spinning
and some will be just chilling.
Starting at the beginning with aunt **A**.
She has been rather sick, so we pray
that soon she will be able to tell
everyone that she is happy and well.

Next is uncle **B** who likes to go
and watch the cowboy rodeo.
He enjoys playing his banjo
with his friend Navaho Joe.

Now cousin **C** is a real star.
For a rock band she plays her guitar.
She bought herself a red jaguar
because she has to travel so far.

The twin girls **I** and **Y**,
you know the ones that are so shy.
Their mother is the one named **D**
who enjoys listening to a rhapsody

Mrs. **E** she loves to cook and bake.
She is famous for her carrot cake.

Her only son **F**, he is a mime.
He will work for only a dime.

The Reverend **G** is one to behold,
when the baby Jesus story is told.
He says this story all should read,
and then wishes everyone Godspeed.

Uncle **H** went to Spain.
First, he went on a plane,
then he took a train
over some very rough terrain.

We told you about the brothers two.
The ones who work in the zoo.
You know, the twins **J** and **K**.
The ones that live by the bay.

What happened to the sisters **I** and **Y**?
It is funny that you should ask why.
For you may think they are at play,
no, they're wrapping presents for Christmas day.

Great grandpapa **L** was a pioneer.
Some say he is as old as King Lear.
One Christmas Eve did appear,
to him, Santa and his reindeer.

Now grandpa **M** had very little hair.
But almost everything he can repair.
Some say he was as good as a saint
because he never had a complaint.

Grandpa's younger brother **N** had a glare.
For hours and hours, he could stare.
Relative **O** they say was a millionaire.
It may be true, I don't know, I don't care.

Second cousin **P** there's not a trace.
Last we heard he was running a race.

But cousin **Q** is in a strange place
she's an astronaut in outer space.

Big brother **R** is really brave,
but sometime he can misbehave.
He wants to grow up and be a sailor,
or was it a tailor, or a jailer?

Little brother **S** someday,
would like to basketball play
for the Indiana Pacers.
While in Indy he could see racers.

Sister **T** follows the latest fad,
this makes her happy and glad.
She has a boyfriend, Tad.
I guess that's not so bad.

Older sister they named her **U.**
She is silly and has a pet cockatoo.
Now she is in college at Purdue
and her boyfriend's name is Hugh.

Younger sister **V** is in high school.
Her favorite color is blue.
Her report card we were all amazed,
for straight A's, she was praised.

Now Ms. **W** how she could chat.
She wore such a funny hat.
She used to be a circus acrobat,
until she got too fat.
Did I tell you about the cousins three?
the mischievous ones **X**, **Y** and **Z?**
They could sing in harmony
and they all knew their geography.

Now **X** was a real dude.
He could be in the strangest mood.
When he became very rude,
he was sent to his room to brood.

Y, her hair she would always comb
and bore you with her trip to Rome.
Z was somewhat eccentric,
but she was very energetic.

Now you have met the Alpha family;
A, B, C, D, E, F, G,
H, I J, K, L, M, N, O, P,
Q, R, S, T, U, V, W, X, Y and **Z.**

Every year the family would meet.
no matter the weather; rain, snow or sleet.

Of one Christmas Eve they do not speak.
The time Santa almost did not stop for a peek

It was Christmas Eve, Eve.
The night before Christmas Eve.
Now this warning, do take heed,
any further you may not want to read.

So that it will not be misleading,
this story we will not be fleeing.
But, talking in rhyme we will leave,
to finish a story, you may disbelieve.

A pause we will now take,
so, an exit you may make,
before we tell this secret story.
To stay and listen is not mandatory.

It was Christmas Eve, Eve. Mother **D**, aunt **A** and Mrs. **E** were busy in the kitchen preparing the Christmas Eve and Christmas day meals and snacks.

The aroma from the kitchen was delightful, and tempting, as the children would sneak in to steal a bite of the goodies.

The homemade chocolate bon bon's were everyone's favorite. You could smell the turkey and all its fixings. Fresh rolls and carrot cake were being baked in the oven

Some of the younger girls were helping to make the Swedish meatballs. Everyone was having fun preparing for the days to come.

Most of the children were sledding in the park. Except for the cousins three. You know **X**, **Y**, and **Z**, they were in the back yard having a snowball fight.

Great grandpapa was napping in his easy chair and grandpa was reading stories to the little ones. Uncle's **B** and **H** were helping **U** and **R** decorate the tree. Everyone was having a grand time. Now and then you would hear someone sing a Christmas song.

The neighbor, Ms. **W**, stopped by with her plate of cookies and a merry Christmas for everyone. The Reverend **G** came by to wish everyone God speed and joined in a Christmas song or two.

Everyone was looking forward with excitement to Christmas Eve and the celebration of Jesus' birth by giving presents to all. The Christmas tree would be surrounded with presents and some of the bigger presents were hidden in closets.

Then it happened! Loud voices came from the other room. It was the twins **I** and **Y** arguing. Their voices got louder and louder. Finally, uncle **B** went into the room to see what was the matter.

Uncle **B** shouted to everyone to come into the room. The children were arguing whether Santa Claus was real or not? If so, how could he bring toys to all the girls and boys in the world? And, why didn't he stop at **I**'s friend's house last year?

Well, the argument got quite heated. Finally, Uncle **H** said "Let us ask grandpa, he should know." So, they went to grandpa and asked him the question. "Is Santa Claus real? How does he bring toys to all the girls and boys in the world?"

Well grandpa got a puzzled look on his face. He thought for a few moments. Then he said "I know, let's wake up great grandpapa and ask him. He once met Santa and his reindeer".

So, the whole group; Aunt **A**, Uncle **B**, cousin **C**, mother **D**, Mrs. **E**, Mrs. E's son **F**, the Rev. **G**, uncle **H**, grandpa **M**, grandpa's brother **N**, big brother **R**, older sister **U**, and younger sister **V** and the twins **I** and **Y** went into the room where great grandpapa was napping.

"You wake him up," said uncle **H** to uncle **B**. "No way!" replied uncle **B**. I think grandpa would be best to wake great grandpapa", stated the Rev. **G**.

So gently grandpa nudged great grandpapa until he wakened. Great grandpapa's big eyes rolled opened to find the room filled with the Alpha family and their guests. He rubbed his eyes and he said "What on earth is going on?"

"There has been a big argument great grandpapa" said mother **D**, "we need your wisdom to help us understand. Is Santa Claus real? If so, how does he bring toys to all the girls and boys in the world?" "Ho, ho, ho, ho," laughed great grandpapa, "What a funny family I have. Let me tell you this way;"

Yes, there is a man in red,
who has a great big magic sled.

Even when the earth freezes.
he can go as fast as he pleases.

Every year he celebrates the noel.
Listen close and you can hear his bell.
While you sleep open an ear,
so, his magic reindeer you will hear.

Do not give this old man a jeer.
For many a boy and girl have shed a tear.
So real or not, give him a hey,
for the happiness he brings on this day

Whether you are young or grown,
let this truth be known.
Santa only comes on Christmas Eve.
To the people who believe.

So spread the Christmas cheer,
you will be surprised who will appear.
Let us all stop and pray,
for peace on earth this Christmas day.

"So, do you believe?" asked great grandpapa.

All the Alpha family did believe. On Christmas Eve there
were presents galore under the Alpha family Christmas tree.

What a mess did occur when all the presents were unwrapped. There were songs of Christmas joy and soon the children were all tired and went to bed. What a great day!

"Where is great grandpapa?" asked cousin **C**. "I think he went outside," said uncle **B**, "to check on his ten-year-old dog Fleck."

THE END

THE LAND OF THERE ONCE WAS

(Or do miracles still really happen?)
(Madelyn's Story)

Now you may think that this is a silly story,
about strange and funny territory.
It is written about **the land of there once was.**
A land that was about to disband.

This story is to remind us of the reason,
for celebrating the Christmas season.
Shall we begin our story new,
for Madyjo from Papa Lou?

This story was given in a poem, to Papa by
a gnome.
It may not make sense, because it was told
under a dome.

It was quite a sight, when Papa was driving
one night,
from Indiana to Tennessee until dawns early
light.

Now here is the poem, written by the gnome,
under the dome.
It's not too long. Can you make it into a song?

*(Do you know what a gnome is? A gnome is a
little old man living under a bridge.)*

There once was a mouse, she lived in a hat.
Her neighbor was fat, she was a white cat.
There once was a rat, who lived in a flat.
His neighbor was black, it was a big bat.

There once was a fox, she lived in a box.
Her neighbors were nice, a family of mice.
There once was a dog, he lived in a log.
It was the same tree, were lived Mr. Bee.

There once was a squeaky squirrel,
he could dance and he could twirl.
There once was a dog named BeeZee,
he would take everything really easy.

There once was a snake, who lived by a lake.
Friends he could not make, except for a big
stake.

There once was a duck, who lived in a truck,
until the lottery she won, what luck!

There once was a goose, who lived with a
moose.
They lived in the forest, just running loose.
There once was a bee, who lived in a tree.
Her neighbor was me; can't you see?

There once was an old man, he lived in a
garbage can.
He played in a band and his name was just Dan.

There once was a bat, who lived in a top hat.
His friends name was Matt, a mischievous cat.

There once was a nice young boy named Bo,
who jumped high one day and broke his toe.
There once was a pretty angel blue.
Whose power so much good she could do.

There once was a bear, who would always take
a dare.
then one day on a dare, he lost all of his hair.
(Have you ever seen a hairless bear?)

There once was a turkey, his name was perky.
He lived by a river that was very murky.
There once was a deer, she looked in a mirror
and frighten herself away, O' dear!

There once was a goat who lived on a boat.
and a gray horse, who lived on a golf course.
There once was a robin, who couldn't stop
sobbin,
because on her foot there was a yellow bobbin.

There once was a hare, who lived on a
mountain top.
He could jump and he could run, his name was
hoppity hop.
There once was a butterfly, she lived way up
in the sky.
She had no neighbors because she lived too
high.

There once was a seal, who loved every meal.
For food he was always willing to make a deal.
There once was a rabbit, she had a terrible
habit.
She would get so sick, when she would chew
on cabit.
  (Cabit is a small cabbage)

There once was Desmo and Rufus two
batmasters,
that would fly around and create disasters.
There once was a monk old and wise,
who would sit around all day and advise.

There once was an ant, who said that he can't,
put on his shirt, and a one-legged pant.

There once was a tick, his name was
Sweetlick.
He had a twin brother, whose name was
Beatnik.

There once was a parakeet, who thought she
was pretty neat.
But she could hardly peep, and had such ugly
feet.
There once was a dinosaur, who had a great
big sore,
and because of the sore he could not eat any
more.

There once was a polar bear,
he lived where it was cold everywhere.
One day he took a trip,
and went off to the county fair.

There once was a coyou (ki-oo),
that liven in the bayou,
where you had to know how to swim,
and do a backward diyou.

*(Coyou is a small dog like animal and a diyou
is a flip into the water)*

There once was a beetle, his name was seedle.
He was so small he could walk on a needle.

There once was a fingle, who made up a jingle,
and sold it to Mr. Mingle, or was it Mr. Ringle?

(Fingle a prehistoric creature with finger feet.)

There once was a time, when believing was a
crime.
What was abolished were seesaws and Santa
Claus.
There once was a time at the end of dawn,
when all good days were gone.

You know days like; playdays, birthdays, May days, Sundays,
holidays, Easter days, Saturdays, Christmas days.

"Stop! STOP! STOP!" I hollered. "I can't stand this! What
do you mean there once was a Santa Claus, and all good
days like Christmas are gone?" I asked the gnome.

Then the gnome went on to tell me the story about the **land
of there once was.** There once was a land of sad people that
did not believe. Because they did not believe they did not
trust in each other either. Because they did not trust in each
other they would hide themselves from other people.

People soon stopped seeing each other. They moved
into caves to avoid having any contact with each other.
When there weren't enough caves, they started digging
underground tunnels to live in. There they lived like moles
under the ground.

With no one to take care of the land, the land started to get darker. The sun begins to dim and the moon moved away to another universe. The stars stopped shining, it was the grimmest place any one ever saw, all because no one would believe.

Passing through the **land of there once** was a fine young gentleman named P. Do you remember? He was the cousin of astronaut Q. One hot summer night, while racing, P stopped to rest under a tree.

He noticed three men approaching him. He jumped up and ran to meet and welcome them. "Sirs," he said, "do not run away but come rest with me under the shade of this old oak tree. Sit awhile before continuing your journey." P then shared some of his food and water with them.

The three men and P talked for some time. When P asked them why they journeyed into the **land of there once was** they hesitated to tell him.

"Should we hide our plan from this gentle man." stated one of the men. After they debated among themselves, they decided to inform P of their mission. "We are angels sent from God", explained one of the angels, "to carry out a special mission."

Well, this just got P's curiosity up and he persisted on knowing the purposes of the angel's mission. "To learn of our mission may upset you," said one of the angels. "Are you sure you really want to know?" "Yes," replied P, hesitantly. "Then You shall Know," remarked the angels.

So, the angel told P; "We have heard that the people of the **land of there once was** no longer believe and that the land is going dark. We have come to see if these reports are true. If so, it is our job then to shut down this land forever."

P sat there stunned, and in utter disbelief. When P finally regained his poise, he approached the angels. "Will you destroy all those who believe as well as all those who do not believe?" asked P. "Yes." replied the angels.

Then P pleaded" Suppose you can find fifty people who believe. Would you not spare the **land of there once was** for them? Surely it would be unfair to destroy the believers too. That wouldn't be fair!" continued P.

The angels thought for a while and then replied to P; "If we find fifty people who believe we will spare the **land of there once was**."

P asked again; "Suppose there are only thirty people who believe would you still spare the **land of there once was**?" Again, the angels thought and replied; "If we find thirty people who believe we will spare the **land of there once was**."

Finally, P asked one more time; "Suppose there are only ten people who believe would you spare the **land of there once was**." The angels thought and thought and then they stated; "Ok, for the sake of just ten people who believe we will spare the **land of there once was**."

Then the angels went on their way and P continued his race, with a tear in his eye, for he feared that the angels would not find ten people who believed in the **land of there once was**.

Now, in the **land of there once was**, was a little girl named Madyjo. She was an orphan girl that had been adopted by a wealthy couple, Namen and Naomi.

They had a huge house on a large estate with many workers to help them keep up the house and their estate. Namen and Naomi had no children before they adopted Madyjo.

Madyjo learned to do many new things in her new home and she soon learned to love her new parents. She especially liked to help them around their house and working in their vegetable garden.

One day, after Madyjo had lived with her new parents for a while, she found her mother looking very sad. She wanted to give comfort to her, so she asked her mother what was troubling her. Madyjo learned that her new father had a deadly disease and was dying.

Madyjo started to tell Naomi about some things her birth mother told her before her death. It was about believing in Christmas, angels and stuff. Madyjo tried hard to remember all the things her birth mother had taught her.

Naomi and Madyjo talked for some days, on and off, about believing and the power of prayer to bring about miracles through believing. They shared this information with the workers too.

Naomi had a talk with Namen about the things they had been discussing. "Where can I find these angels and people who work miracles?" asked Namen, "I shall give them gold and silver to make me well." "They don't take gold and silver" stated, Madyjo, "to receive their gifts all you have to do is believe."

Madyjo went on to explain how her birth mother told her how to pray and ask God for His blessings and help. When her mother died Madyjo prayed that she would get a new mother and that she could have a father too. Well; she told Naomi and Namen that when they adopted her and took her into their home all her prayers were answered.

Namen was a proud man and he had some doubts in what Madyjo was saying. It just didn't seem right that someone would just give something so valuable away as a miracle.

For a little girl Madyjo showed great wisdom. For she tried to explain to her father that the secret of receiving a miracle is just that; you must trust and believe, that a miracle is a free gift.

Just like Christmas, Santa Claus, the Blue Angel and the baby Jesus, these are all miracles in their own way and are a free gift to all that believe.

The enjoyment of miracles is not casting doubt upon them but rather receiving them as gifts. If you doubt, you will not be able to enjoy and receive the gift.

This is what is happening to the **land of there once was**. People stopped believing. After listening to Madyjo's words, Naman was moved. He gathers Naomi, Madyjo and the workers.

They all kneeled down. Trusting and believing they began a prayer. Little did they know how that prayer changed the **land of there once was** forever, as three angels were walking by their home.

THE END

Printed in the United States
by Baker & Taylor Publisher Services